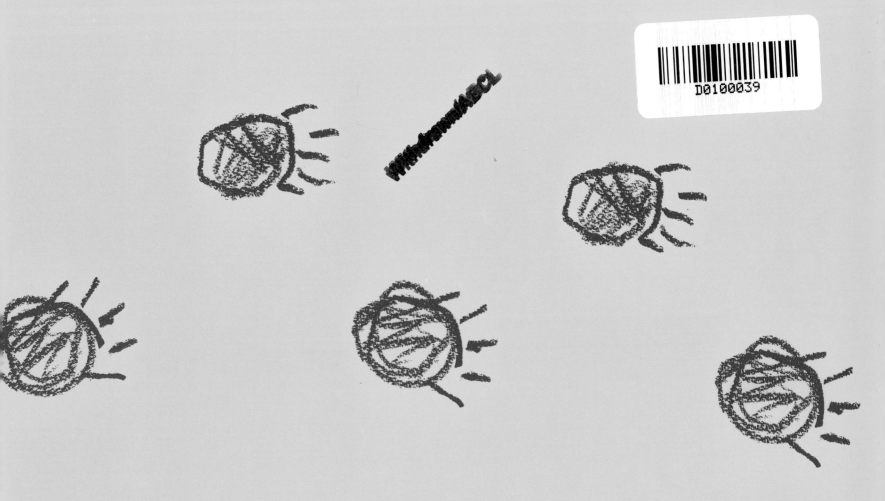

YOU'RE A BEAR

For Lenorala
—M.J.

For Tyler
—S.J. & L.F.

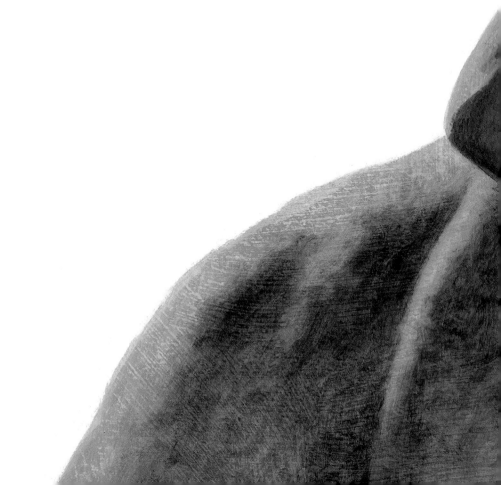

YOU'RE A
BEAR

by
Mavis Jukes

paintings by
Steve Johnson and **Lou Fancher**

Alfred A. Knopf   New York

You're a gruff bear, with fleas—
a grump, with a hump between your shoulders.
Scramble from your hidden ledge—
hidden by a bramble hedge—
and squeeze between the boulders.

Ramble through the midnight breeze.

Then—freeze!

You're a bold bear

with a nose as cold as cheese.

Slyly rise up on your toes.
Sniff for owl in the skies—
whiff for mountain goat or moose on the loose
or lynx on the prowl.

Or bees in the trees . . .

Thrash a clump of shrubs for berries!

Rip up rotten logs for grubs!

Check your feet and paws.

There's a chance that

in your fur might

be a termite.

Nibble ants between your claws.

Wish for fish. Stand in the sand
by a stream.
In a pool you'll see reflections of your drool.
You'll see floppy lips—and underneath,
scary teeth that gleam and glimmer.

Above your ears the moon will tip and sink into
a cloud and shimmer
as you dip and drink. And dunk your snout.
Shake those hairy hips to spook the trout!
Then drip and dribble out.

You're a huffy bear. You've missed fish—but
had a wash.
So now you're a fluffy bear.
And all the moonlit meadow grass is yours to
squish and squash.

Spin and tumble.

Sit and sing, or grumble.

Lie back and rest.

Above your furry chest

stars wink.

Dawn leaks blurry shades of peach

and streaks of pink. The moon fades.

Yawn. S ~ t ~ r ~ e ~ t ~ c ~ h those toes!

Reach above your mighty nose and tongue!

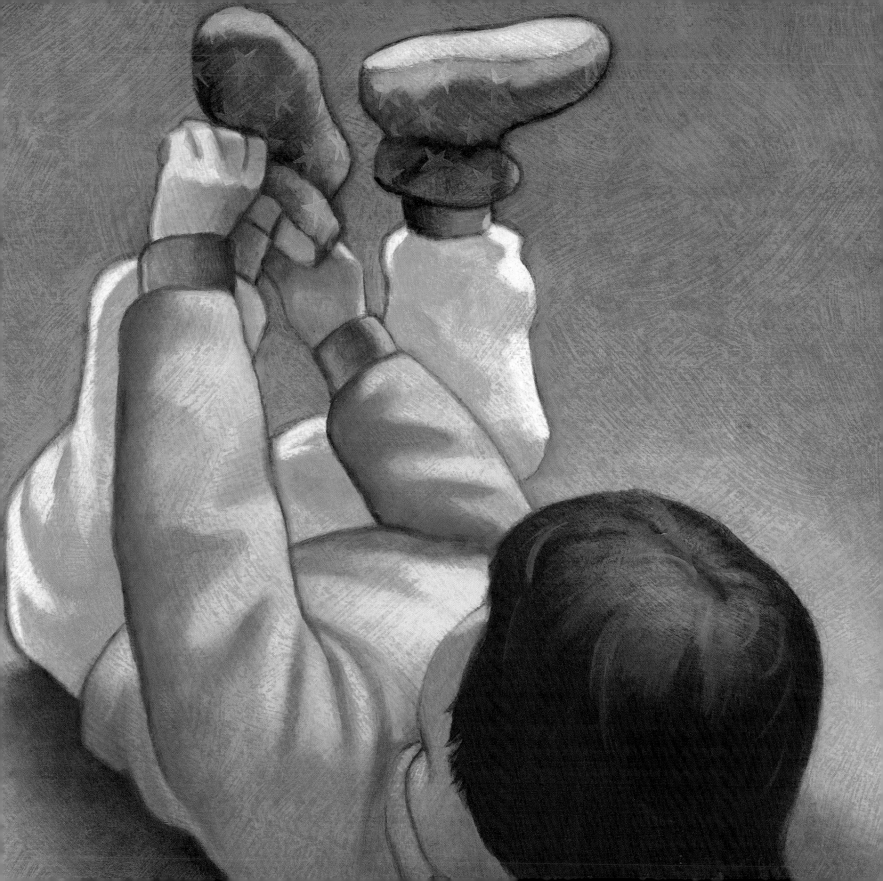

You're a tired grizzly—
who's dizzily spun and sung,
who's busily eaten rows of unhatched flies,
made footprints on the beach unmatched in size.

Soon the sun will rise on the horizon.

Eyes glitter in the woods and blink;
they're watching you, the groggy grizzly
who's snooped and snacked and had a drink.
And gotten soggy.
And now is pooped and ready to roam home.

You're a bear who rustles
deep in fallen leaves to rest
your muscles.
Lumber to your hidden lair to slumber.

Choose a soft and mossy place
to couch that glossy nose
and woolly face
so you can doze.

Close
your eyes.
Your ribs will slowly fall and rise.

Above your tail an owl flies
into dim, pale, powdery skies.

Below, a mountain goat or moose will march
and snort and arch his throat
to tip his rack and bellow—
a lynx will slouch her back
and prowl and squint her yellow eyes,
and crouch. And scream!

But you, the fearless bear, will dream.

There's a hush of wind;
it ruffles your hair.
The air grows still.
You're a grizzly bear
asleep on a hill
on the edge of the world
in the brush
on a ledge,
with your paws curled.

THIS IS A BORZOI BOOK PUBLISHED BY ALFRED A. KNOPF

www.randomhouse.com/kids

Library of Congress Cataloging-in-Publication Data
Jukes, Mavis.
You're a bear / by Mavis Jukes ; illustrated by Steve Johnson and Lou Fancher. — 1st ed.
p.   cm.
Summary: A young girl pretends she is a bear roaming through the night.
ISBN 0-375-80267-3 (trade) — ISBN 0-375-90267-8 (lib. bdg.)
[1. Imagination—Fiction. 2. Bears—Fiction. 3. Stories in rhyme.]
I. Johnson, Steve, 1960– ill. II. Fancher, Lou, ill. III. Title.
PZ8.3.J845Yo 2003
[E]—dc21
2003040072

Book design by Lou Fancher

Printed in the United States of America
September 2003

10 9 8 7 6 5 4 3 2 1
First Edition

Mavis Jukes

is the author of *Like Jake and Me*, a Newbery Honor Book. Her other books include *I'll See You in My Dreams*, *Blackberries in the Dark*, *It's a Girl Thing*, *Growing Up: It's a Girl Thing*, and *The Guy Book*. She has two adult daughters and two adult stepsons and lives in Northern California with her husband, artist Robert Hudson.

Steve Johnson & Lou Fancher

have collaborated on a number of notable children's books, including *New York's Bravest* by Mary Pope Osborne, *My Many Colored Days* by Dr. Seuss, *The Salamander Room* by Anne Mazer, *The Frog Prince, Continued* by Jon Scieszka, *Robin's Room* by Margaret Wise Brown, and *Bambi*, retold by Janet Schulman. Steve and Lou live in Minneapolis, Minnesota, with their son, Nicholas.

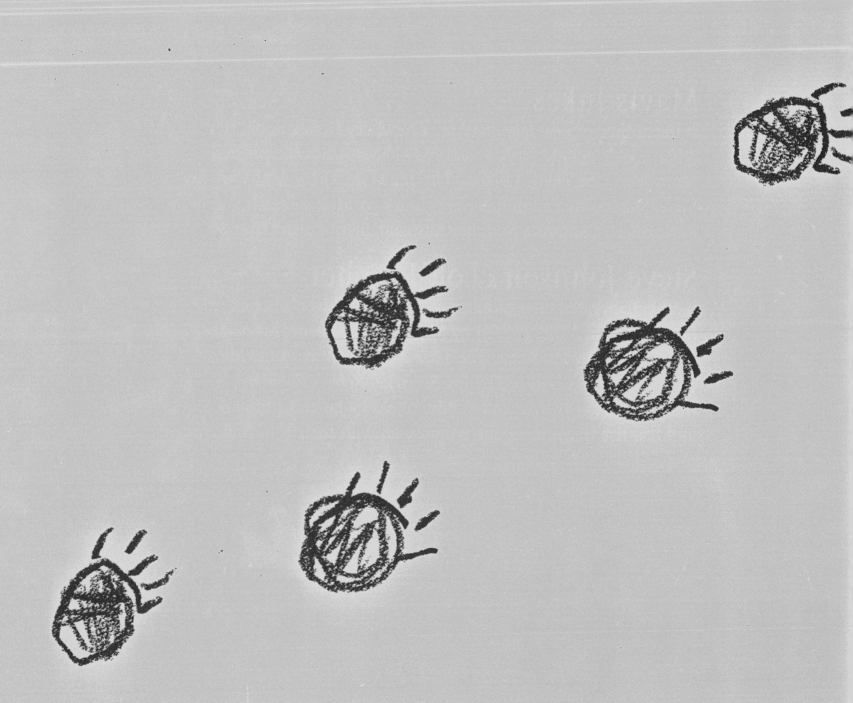